Animals on Parade

Collection © 2006 Bayard Canada Books Inc.
Rhymes and illustrations © authors and illustrators

Publisher: Jennifer Canham
Editorial Director: Mary Beth Leatherdale
Assistant Editor: David Field
Production Manager: Lesley Zimic
Production Editor: Larissa Byj
Production Assistant: Kathy Ko

Design: Blair Kerrigan/Glyphics

Special thanks to Katherine Dearlove, Barb Kelly, and Brenda Halliday, Librarian, The
Canadian Children's Book Centre.

We gratefully acknowledge the financial support of the Government of Canada through
the Book Publishing Industry Development Program (BPIDP) for our publishing activities.

 Conseil des Arts   Canada Council
du Canada   for the Arts

Library and Archives Canada Cataloguing in Publication

Animals on parade : favourite rhymes from Chirp magazine / Mary Beth
Leatherdale, ed.

ISBN 2-89579-119-8
ISBN 978-2-89579-119-5

1. Children's poetry, Canadian (English) 2. Children's stories, Canadian (English).
3. Canadian poetry (English)–20th century. 4. Canadian fiction (English)–20th century.
I. Leatherdale, Mary Beth

PS8231.A54 2006   jC810.8'09282   C2006-903569-5

Acknowledgements:
"The Dinosaur Dinner" appears from *Dinosaur Dinner* (Alfred A. Knopf, 1997).
© 1997 Dennis Lee. With permission of the author.

"To Market" illustration by Barbara Reid was photographed by Ian Crysler.

Every effort has been made to locate the copyright holders of materials used in this book.
Should there be any omissions or errors, we apologize and shall be pleased to make the
appropriate acknowledgements in future editions.

Printed in Canada

Owlkids Publishing
10 Lower Spadina Ave., Suite 400
Toronto, Ontario M5V 2Z2
Ph: 416-340-2700
Fax: 416-340-9769

Distributed by UTP Distribution

From the publisher of

CHirp   chickaDEE   OWL

Visit us online!
www.owlkids.com

Animals on Parade

Favourite Rhymes from Chirp Magazine

Owl kids

Thinking Happy Thoughts

I love the holes in donuts,
You can stick your fingers through.
I love to splash in puddles,
Squishing mud-delicious goo.
When I'm itchy I love scratching,
I love picking at my scabs.
Lots of chocolate makes me smile,
So does my chocolate lab.

I like chairs when they're upside down,
My tents are excellent!
Banging pots and pans is fun
Until the spoon is bent.
I love rocks in all my pockets,
New sneakers when they squeak.
I love when no one's talking
And I get a chance to speak.

I like cracking ice in puddles,
Spider web designs!
I love a birthday party
When the presents are all mine.
I love blowing big pink bubbles,
I love to crinkle cans.
What makes me happiest of all?
Today?
Holding daddy's hand.

Sheree Fitch
Illus.: Céline Malépart

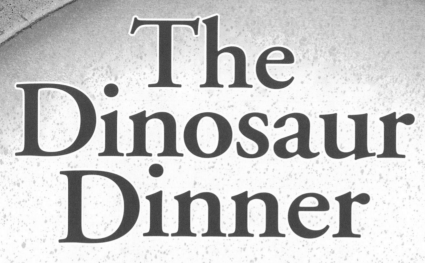

The Dinosaur Dinner

Allosaurus, stegosaurus,
Brontosaurus too,
All went off for dinner at the
Dinosaur zoo;

Along came the waiter, called
Tyrannosaurus Rex,
Gobbled up the table
'Cause they wouldn't pay their checks.

Dennis Lee
Illus.: John Berg